This Book Belongs to

For Julie – PS
For my parents, John and Margaret – JP

First published in Great Britain and in the USA in 2016 by Otter-Barry Books,
Little Orchard, Burley Gate, Herefordshire, HR1 3QS
This paperback edition first published in Great Britain by Otter-Barry Books in 2017

A catalogue record for this book is available from the British Library.

ISBN 978-1-910959-04-6

Illustrated with collage

Printed in China

1 3 5 7 9 8 6 4 2

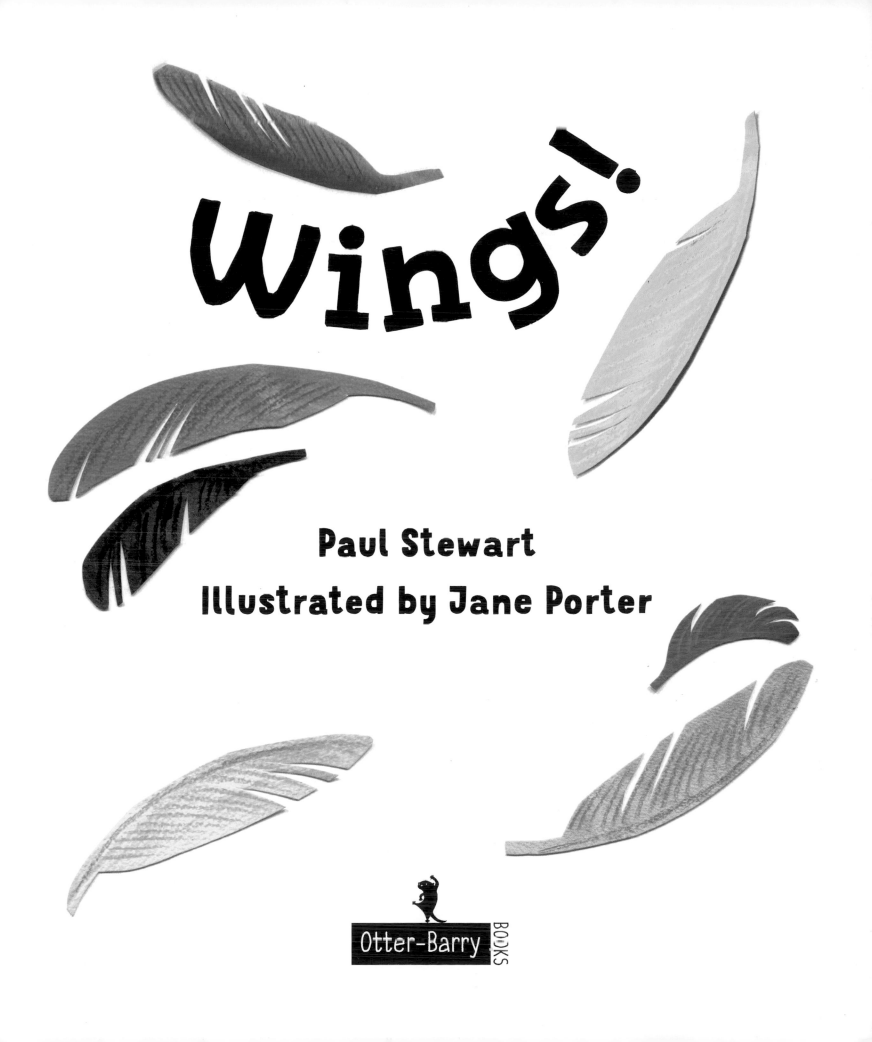

Wings!

Paul Stewart

Illustrated by Jane Porter

Otter-Barry BOOKS

Everyone was having fun at the Grand Gathering of the Birds.

Then someone shouted, "Last one to the top of the tree's a rotten egg!"

There was screeching and squawking and a flapping of wings...

And suddenly Penguin was all on his own. **AGAIN.**

"I **wish** I could fly," he said to himself sadly.

"I'll teach myself to fly,"
said Penguin.

He tried...

and tried...

and tried,

and tried,

and tried...

But nothing worked.

"I'll get my friends to help me,"
Penguin decided.

"Wurrrgh..."

"What have you been doing?" asked Ostrich.
"Your beak's all wonky."

"Trying to fly," said Penguin.

Ostrich sniffed. "I've always found
flying a little... common," he said.
"Walking is so much more dignified."

"I couldn't agree more," said Emu.

"All that flapping and fluttering nonsense."

"It makes me **dizzy** just to think about it," said Kiwi. "I've **never** liked heights."

"But I've **always** dreamed of flying," said Penguin. "From the day I first hatched. It's my deepest desire. My destiny..."

"You look down in the beak," said Parrot.
"You look down in the beak."

"I wish I could fly," said Penguin.
"And I can't."

"Practice makes perfect," said Parrot.
"Practice makes perfect."

"Not always," said Penguin.
"And it's making me so sad."

"Laughter is the best medicine," said Parrot. "Why does Stork stand on one leg?"

"Don't know," said Penguin.

"Because he'd fall over if he lifted the other one," said Parrot.

Penguin nodded politely.

"Am I cheering you up?" asked Parrot.
"Not really," said Penguin.

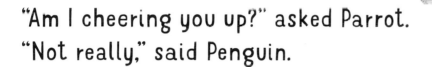

Parrot flew off.
Penguin watched him.
"I **wish** I could fly," he said.

"I shall teach you to fly," said Owl.

Penguin learned how to flap.

Penguin learned how to jump and flap.

Penguin learned how to run and jump and flap.

"How am I doing?" asked Penguin.

"I've seen better," Owl replied.

Penguin watched Swallow darting after insects.

He watched Robin fluttering from branch to branch.

He watched Blue Tit hovering as he pecked at berries.

He watched Goose gliding over the lake.

A **BIG fat tear** ran down Penguin's beak and dripped to the ground.

Suddenly, there was a great commotion.
The sky was full of birds.

There was Owl,
with Sparrow and Starling
and Duck and Flamingo
and Eagle
and Parrot and Hummingbird
and Swan
and Swallow
and Robin
and Blue Tit
and Goose.
And **ALL** of them were flying.

"I wish I could fly!"
Penguin called up to them.

"And so you shall!" they called back,
long pieces of string unrolling from their beaks.
"Tie the string around you and hold on!"

Penguin felt like a trussed-up parcel.
There was a lurch and a jolt,
and the string went taut.
Then...

Up he soared.

Below him were fields and woods
and streams.
Villages and farms.
The sea.

Suddenly, Penguin was not flying.
He was falling.

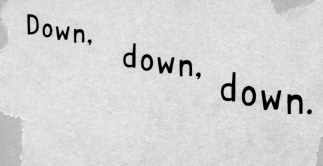

Down,   down,   down.

SPLASH!

into the water.

Penguin kicked his legs

and flapped his wings.

He soared, he swooped, he dived.

He darted, he fluttered,

he hovered, he glided –

then he flew back towards the air.

The birds were flapping and fluttering above him.
They looked concerned.

"Sorry we dropped you!" said Owl.

"That's all right," said Penguin. "If you hadn't
dropped me, I would never have learned."

"What did you learn?" the birds called back.

And Penguin flew back
to the bottom of the ocean,
with his wings taking him

all the way

down!

About the Author and Illustrator

Paul Stewart is an award-winning author of books for children of all ages – everything from picture books to football stories, fantasy and horror. Internationally acclaimed, his books have been translated into over 30 languages. Together with Chris Riddell, he is the co-creator of the *Far-Flung Adventure* series, which include *Fergus Crane*, Gold Smarties Prize Winner, *Corby Flood* and *Hugo Pepper*, Silver Nestlè Prize Winners, as well as the *Edge Chronicles* series, which has sold over two million books worldwide. Paul lives in Brighton with his wife.

• • •

Jane Porter is a children's book illustrator who loves working with ink, paint and collage. She has also worked on illustration commissions for organisations such as London Zoo, the National Trust, Kensington Palace and the V&A. Her baby book *This Rabbit, That Rabbit* was chosen by BookTrust for the Bookstart scheme in 2015, and her first book as both author and illustrator, *Pink Lion*, was published in 2017. Jane lives and works in London.

www.janeporter.co.uk